FOR BIG, MY FATHER,MY BEST FRIEND, MY ANGEL. THANK
YOU FOR EVERYTHING   POP. MAY YOU REST IN PEACE.
I LOVE YOU.
 C.A.K.E IS FICTION ANY NAMES OR PLACES ARE STRICTLY
CIRCUMSTANCES. IT IS A WORK OF ART CREATED BY THE
AUTHOR TO BRING INSIGHT INTO THE PLACES HE HAS LIVED

AND THE LIFE HE HAS OVERCOME. IT IS RAW AND IS INTENDED TO BE RAW AND TO REMAIN RAW. IT WAS WRITTEN AS IF IT WAS BEING TOLD TO YOU BY AN ORDINARY GUY FROM THE HOOD. IT HAS SPELLING ERAS AND SOME GRAMMATICAL ERAS THAT ARE INTENTIONALLY IGNORED TO GIVE YOU THE RAW FEELING. SO WITH AN OPEN MIND ENJOY THE 1ST OF A SERIES OF SHORT STORIES WRITTEN BY I AM SALADEEN. AUDIO BOOKS AND A ANIMATED SERIES ARE IN THE WORKS . AS A 1ST TIME AUTHOR THIS IS JUST THE BEGINNING. ENJOY

2

COMING SOON...... C.A.K.E II MORE CAKE (CAN'T ALWAYS KEEP EVERYTHING) DEC 2017
ALSO LOOK FOR THE AUDIO AND ANIMATED SERIES COMING SOON ,I AM SALADEEN

C.A.K.E.

CASH ADDICTED KIDS EATIN

STORY 1
PART 1

C.A.K.E.

"The Picture"

"Damn... a nigga need a fuckin come up." Kills mumbled to himself as he walked thru the projects, leaving the bodega getting loosies and dutches.

Kills was a nickname giving to him by his childhood friends. It was actually short for Shaquille. His father was a huge LSU fan and named him after Shaquille O'Neil.

"Yoooooo... what's popping homie"? Kills heard a familiar voice say from the other side of the street. "Yoooo ...what's good Big Homie" he replied, as he crossed the street and began to realize exactly who had spoken to him.

"Oooohhh shit Butter... what's popping B"? Kills asked as he extended his hand to greet the OG.

"Niggas like u lil homie...what's the word on da curb"? He replied smoothly. See OG Butter wasn't ya ordinary nigga...6'4, dark as night and had the body of a lineman. He kept his hair in that Puffy S curl look. Neatly trimmed and styled into a fade. No facial hairs and

4

his mouth almost looked like a chipmunk. But he wasn't called "Butter" for his looks obviously, but instead for his smooth way of talking and dressing. Butter could sell you a dream, wake you up in the middle, and resell the same dream like it's new. He had the gift of gab since he could speak. You never seen Butter in anything less than the latest. Sneakers jeans hats jerseys you name it Butter had it.

But the main reason he was called "Butter" was in the early crack era days he was no more than 12 ..13 and he found some coke in his Grandmother building. He cooked it up into crack but when it came back it had a yellow tint to it ...kind of like Butter. He hit da block and said "I got that Butter " and the rest is history........

"Naw OG you got it I jus want it..."Kills fired back. Kills was somewhat of a wordsmith himself.

"I'm out here tryna get it when I do we can split it" the OG spewed.

Kills laughed knowing he wasn't ready for this niggas wordplay and rebuttals, so he changed the subject.

"Nigga u sharp as a thumbtack...where you goin court or a funeral "? He asked referring to the dress clothes Butter was rockin.

"Lil nigga that ain't the only reasons to get grown man, wit ya gear.... but I jus left court." He replied in a joking manner. As they laughed at the OGs joke a screen door open and a light skinned girl with long hair stuck her head out and said, "Shaquille stop talkin so damn loud. I can hear ya mouth way upstairs buzzo "

Kills looked away from his OG and said " daaammnnnnn Gigi why u callin a nigga government like dat"?

"Nigga every fuckin body know ya real name.... "Kills". besides we family. Sup Butter you coming in to grab that or no"? She asked dismissing Kills." Hold on.. y'all know each other "? Kills asked not going away so easy.

"Yea lil homie u kno I'm in tuned with everyone everywhere..when I need to be." Butter answered.

"That's bonkers ..small world B" Kills said.   "But imma get up with y'all man lemme get to the spot "

"Ayo take my number u tryna get some bread let me know I might gotta spot for you. Jus holla at me YG" YG what he called all the lil homies, it stood for "Young Gangsta".

"Say less OG" he replied thinking "damn that shit on time". After getting Butters math and hugging his cousin he headed home. While walking he was thinking bout last week's convo wit another OG.

 Hi Face.   "What's goody lil homie...

I got the grams fa you fuck wit me ..know imma look out", Hi proposed to Kills.

"Man, I'm fucked up G... tryna get it", he told the older hustler.

"Shit well you get some paper come check me I'll give you a hustle play", he promised his lil partner. A hustle play was a double up. You spend 20 you get 40 worth. Coming back to reality he realized he was almost to his building. As he approached he started thinking.His mind started to paint a picture of the future.. he saw it so clearly. It was like a premonition. He knew his come up was near. He knew that he would soon be eating. He smiled at the ideal as he twisted the bottom doors knob and headed upstairs.

He was excited how this came together..."Finally" he whispered to no one "Cake"....

CAKE

"Love It When a Plan Comes Together"

"Damn nigga it takes ah hour to go get loosies now"? Sasha questioned Kills.

"No .. but I stopped and was talkin to Butter... the big homie..."he answered back.

"Yea ..ok nigga .. think I'm a dumb bitch? Keep fuckin playin Shaquille you gon b living wit dat bitch"!!Sash shot back. "What bitch Sash? The bitch at the store "? He asked sarcastically as he went to the bed room to get his haze.

"Where the weed at Sash"? He asked his baby's mother sternly.

6

"I put up so ya baby wouldn't get it. It's on the dresser." She answered rolling her eyes.

Kills located his stash and grabbed a Barney and Friends DVD and begin to break up the sticky Purple Haze he copped yesterday from the Spanish lady across the street.

"Really nigga ARE YOU FUCKIN SERIOUS"!!!! He heard Sasha scream from the bathroom. "So you jus gon roll up on Stank movie"?

"Man, she don't use the case ...besides I'll wipe it off. Fuck. make a fuckin big deal bout every fuckin lil ass damn thing man", Kills shot back aggravated.

"Well it's a million fuckin dvds but you pick this one" she said snatching the DVD off his lap causing the weed to scatter all over the table his lap and carpet.

Without warning Kills jumped up grabs Sash by her wrists and moves her out his way before storming out the door. "Might as well take ya shit too bitch ass nigga! Imma telling my brother you put ya hands on my too. he gon fuck ya pussy ass up"!!! She promised. Kills ignored her and kept walking down the stairs fuming.

"I swear I hate this bitch B"!! He said to himself "Always manage to fuck up a good thing. Now Ian got no weed bread nothing. Somn gotta give B" he continued talking to himself as he walked towards the Papi spot to see if he can get a bag on credit.

"Paaapppiiiii what's popping my guy"? Kills greeted the Dominican with excitement hoping he return the energy. "Keels my friend. qua pasa"? He said just as excited to see his customer so soon.

"Ain't shit Juney, but I need a favor Papi" Kills replied desperately. "I need like ah 3,5 till later..you know I got you Papi " he pleaded. "Keels ....ju know i fucks witchoo ,but imma need my money today mang. Ju feel me"? He asked rhetorically. Kills instantly lit up and was filled with a sense of relief."Shit might be looking up after all" he thought. But all he said was "No doubt Papi you already know I gotchu ".

As Junito went into his building to get what Kills asked, Kills thought about where he would post up until Sasha cool off. With no weed it could take awhile."Bitch better pick that shit out the rug and smoke it" he said laughing to himself.

"Here ju go mang". Junito's heavy Dominican accent brought him back to reality. "Good lookin Pa-Pa .. I got you later on tonight ..if not first thing in the am, cool"?

"Ok mang ,jus call me imma be on da west side ".

7

Kills walked off feeling accomplished and ready to smoke. "Damn ..I need a Dutch ."he told the air. As he headed to the store he started putting a plan together. Sell 2 grams keep 1. As he walked into the store he knew he would be more relaxed after smoking.

"Peace Ahk" he greeted the Muslim man behind the counter.

"Good Brother... back already"? The Muslim man questioned. "Yea man a I need a vanilla Dutch Ahk...matter fact lemme jus owe u fa da box of 4 till later. Know I'm good for it"? He said pleading his case knowing it was a shot in the dark." I can't do that you know I would but it's slow today",he answered.

"Man cmo-"

"Iiiiiiiiiiiiiyyyeeee"!!! Kills was interrupted by a loud mouth short brown skinned slim guy, around Kills age."Geeeeeeeeee"!!! Kills replied forgetting about the negotiating he was just doing.

"What's the science my Nigga"? Kills asked the shorter man."You know me my G ...tryna smoke bout to grab these dutchies then run see Billie ".he answered. "Nigga I got some Piff cop one I'll match one". Kills proposed. Without hesitation G excepted and proceeded to purchase the cigars.

"You driving "? Kills asked as they exited the bodega box of cigars in hand.

"You know this my nigga.I keeps the V on go" he said braggingly.

"Take me to State and Dolvin , we can smoke at my buzzo spot."

"Say no more. I'm goin dat way anyway so that works."

As they jumped in Gee's Honda wagon Gee asked "you still mess wit Londa sister"?

"Maaannn ion even wan talk bout this bitch Gee, real nigga shit she the worst EVER"!! He said shaking his head. Gee laughed and Kills joined him and started rollin up for the second time that day.

As they were rolling down State ave Kills zoned out to the 50 Cent that was blaring thru the speakers. "You say you a gangster but you never pop nothing you say you a Wanksta boy you need to stop fronting".

As they approached Kills cousin Max house Gee phone rang."5 minutes" he muttered into the phone. "We match later Kills imma slide through.Lemme get that sack I gotta make dis move" he explained. "IK how that shit goes B, lemme go grab this nigga eyes so I can get you right". He went into Max crib knowing he didn't have a set of eyes but niggas always want they shit off the scale. But Kills could eyeball with the best of em. As he walked outside he saw this Thick yellow bone bent over the passenger side of Gee's whip and instantly the man in him was drawn to her shapely figure. "Well

8

daaayyuuumm ma. All dat jus sittin fatter than a mufucka" he shot. "
Nigga stop playing with me Kills. She said turning around, revealing
her identity. "Damn Connie them beans and rice got you thick" he
said squeezing his home girl. He knew Consuela for a few years his
mom and sisters introduced him to her when he came from
Juvenile.
"Nope fried chicken greens cornbread. You know I hate that
Spanish shit" she said smiling. "Y'all niggas catch up and lemme get
that sack I gotta slide" Gee urged.
 Connie laughed and asked Kills what he was about to do "Shit
smoke and try to get this lil bit of smoke off. What you got shakin'
ma"? He asked her.
 "I'll match you " she offered. "We can go to my crib cuz I wan be
high as fuck and comfortable ". she explained knowing it was at
least 3 other people in the house that smoked. "No doubt ma I'm wit
dat". Kills said
 They started to cross the street and headed towards Connie's
house for the session.
While they smoked and talked Connie asked him. "You know where
I can get some grams"? Kills stopped smoking and looked at her as
if it was the most foreign thing he has ever heard. "Grams what you
need grams for"? He asked ashing the Dutch and relighting it.
 "Man, I need to get this money asap. Shit crazy I got like 30 dollars
I need somn to double up at least." She explained.
 Kills face lit up as his mind began racing at the opportunity that just
fell in his lap. "Ion know off hand but lemme see what I can do ma"
he said knowing Hi was on Hollywood around the corner. And
knowing Hi said he'll look out this was easier than he thought. "Shit
her 30 my 20 I might get at least 2.5" he thought doing the math in
his head.
 "Kills ...Kills ..SHAQUILLE "!!??Connie yelled , her voice cutting
through his daydream like a samurais kitana. "Yo don't call me that
ma...I was jus thinking bout who to link wit.." he said tryna explain
his mental absence from the conversation. "So ...who you thinkin'"?
She urged on.
"You don't know em ma .. but c'mon we bout to hit the strip, grab
that other Dutch". He instructed as he grabbed the rest of the
Piff,and headed towards the front door.
 Little did Kills know this was the beginning of a roller coaster ride
that's filled with twist and turns, but all he saw was CAKE....walking
up Dolvin towards Hollywood he couldn't help but feel a sense of
excitement. He knew he was bout to make some bread. As they

9

turned on Salina ave he saw a purple Ls 460 Lexus parked in front of Charlie's store. "Would you look at this" he muttered to himself. "What you say Pa"? Connie questioned? "Naw nothin ma that's my homie V right there lemme get that bread so I can grab that work". He told her reaching his hand out for the money. "Aight but this shot better be grease nigga" she said meaning the crack better be fire a1 good. "C'mon mami you know better". Kills replies smoothly.

"Faaccceee big homie what it look like my G"? Kills said greeting the plug with love and respect."Nigga it look like money ..everything else lookin funny".. he spat. " Look G I got 50 cent I need that hustle play ". " say no more I told I got you YG... meet me here in 20 minutes imma bring you a lil 3 grammar of some diamond". Hi promised Kills . " Shit imma stay right her and wait". Kills promised "Say no more I'll be right back right back don't move Kills" Hi said seriously. " Nigga I'm posted ya dig", Kills swore as he raised his right hand to insure his seriousness.

CAKE

"Let's get it"

"This shit fuego Hi"? Kills questioned examining the plastic bag containing the work he just purchased."YG, have you ever copped some bs from me"? He asked." Naw ..I'm jus makin sure" ,he replied.
"Vette ..Vette .. cmere " Hi called over a crackhead lady. She was fair skinned dressed in males clothing and was slightly over weight."Sup nephew "? She said shifting her weight from one side to another.
"Tell me what you think bout that new batch I got", he asked her.
"Maaaan that's that shit boy! I'm talkin 88 " she said excitedly remembering the high it gave her.

"Shit reminds me of the good ol days, straight drop" she said dropping down in a squatting pose and bouncing before standing up.
"Yea nigga like I said no bs" Hi said laughing.
"Matter fact I got 6 lemme get a taste " Vette said hoping he accepts the few dollars.
"You want this YG"? He asked Kills.
"Naw I'm bout to make a move lemme see ya jack right quick" Kills replied.
" Yooo what's good OG" Kills said into the Phone.
"YG what's shakin'"? Butters voice boomed from the other side.
"I'm tryna link up. Get this money, I'm on Hollywood where you at"? Kills asked. "I'm caught up right now Imma send Linda to come scoop you don't move YG" Butter said in a serious tone.
"Say no more OG "Kills said hanging up the phone and giving to Hi.
" Good look B, and definitely good look on that hustle play."
" Man don't thank me YG just get CAKE", he said giving Kills a five.
"So, what's good Pa "? Connie questioned as they walked up the street. "Butter bout to send a ride for us. Hi gave me 3 grams so we good ", he explained. A few moments later a grey Buick pulled up and an older white lady with curly salt and pepper hair rolled the window down and said "Kills"?
"Yea that's me, you must be Linda " he said.
"That be me hun" she answered unlocking the door. They climbed into the car and she proceeded to take them to the north side where Butter was waiting ....
They approached the destination on Pond and as they came to the building parking lot a man approached them." Ayo..you good"? The stranger asked.
"What u need "? Kills asked the man.
"50"
"Aite gimmie a sec unk" Kills told the man.
"Ma u know him "? Kills asked Linda
"Yea he be round here begging and doin his lil hustle, he straight ", she informed Kills.
He then proceeded to break the rock down into smaller chunks looking for the perfect rock.
"Here unk ,you gon like that" Kills said handing the man the crack.
"If it's grease imma get witcha" ,the crackhead promised as he skipped off drugs in hand. He didn't get all the way around the building before a lady walked up.
"Where Butter"? She asked anxiously.

"Why what's goody auntie" Kills asked.

" I got 60...but I need somn proper" she said digging in her bra for the cash.

"Ayo what the fuck y'all doin"? Kills recognized the deep voice. " My bad OG we jus pulled up and this shit started clicking", Kills explained to the OG.

"Naw I'm jus fuckin witcha YG .. get that cake lil man. Oh, and here", Butter handed em 2 cell phones "Answer them bitches do numbers " Butter told him.

"Linda take em where the phone tells em, and make sure they good" he instructed the older woman.

"Sure, thing Butter" she assured him.

"When y'all run out go to Lex he got somn fa yall, imma hit y'all later I gotta go do somn .Kills get money YG don't be out here playing" He said firmly before going back in the building.

"Yo"? Kills answered the phone.

"Sup man I need a 50, I'm in the Butternut building" the unfamiliar voice said on the other side.

"10 minutes, be outside" Kills explained. Before they pulled out a light skinned long hair shapely lady came out the building Butter went in. " Sup Pa I'm Cassandra but call me Cassie ", she said getting in the car. They caught the latest sell and then headed to the next. "This shit clickin , like CLICKIN" Kills said not believing the phone was going numbers like that.

"Papi ju jus wait. It's gon go loco",Cassie said In a low voice.

"Man let's get it"

CAKE

"Damn"

"Ecstasy and Desire", Cazz answered her phone in a seductive voice " In call or out call"? She questioned the unknown voice on the other end."90 for half 120 for the full" she said.

"Kills ..you gon answer that"? Connie said referring to the phone Butter gave em. "Oh, shit Ian even hear this shit not used to it yet". He laughed as he answered."Yo"?

"Hey ..Butter said you straight. I need a 30" the voice said.

"Where you at"? Kills asked tapping Linda's leg ready to instruct her where to go. "James Building, you know where that's at "?

"Yea .. 10 minutes" Kills told the voice and hung up.

"Where to darling"? Linda asked.

"James building "he answered

"30" he said to Connie without lookin back, "That's too big mami" Cazz said about the massive size rock Connie had broken off. "This Fuego right? They get a .3 " she explained. "This all " she held up a rock half the size of what Connie was prepared to give the lick."Damn ..that's it? For 30? How you know it's .3"?Connie asked wanting to learn how Cazz eyeballed so well." He estado haciendo esto hace mucho tiempo" she said in their native language. "Ion speak Spanish like that ma", Connie confessed slightly embarrassed. "She said she been doin this a long time "Kills said before Caz opened her mouth "You speaky Spanie"? Cazz asked Kills. "Enough ...I grew up around em" he answered. He grabbed the phone hanging around his neck and redialed the last number. "C'mon" he ordered into the phone.

Before he could hang up the man was walking out the building approaching the car. Kills instantly thought" Dis nigga smoke grease"? As if to read his thoughts Connie said "This nigga smoke grease"?

"I'm thinking the same thing mami" Kills said. "That's Chuck he bien Papi". Cazz assured the couple.

"Oh aite "...Kills said.

Just as they finished putting the work in the bag Chuck approached the passenger side "Sup...Charles...but everyone calls me Chuck", said the neatly dressed and clean-shaven Caucasian man. Kills immediately started analyzing the man. he notices his fingernails were bitten passed the cuticles and his hair though recently cut was a bit disheveled. Big grey eyes that seemed too close together sat above a long sharp pointed nose. Slender somewhat athletic frame was draped in clean office attire.

"She got you my dude go to the back" Kills said directing the man to Connie's window.

"If it's fire I'll be calling you back soon" Chuck promised.

"Guess I'll be talking to you later then" Kills said confidently.

Before they pulled off the phone rang again "Yooo "

"Yea where you at?... Aite 10 minutes "Kills hung up the phone.
"Damn they wanna 100" he said not believing that he just made
$110 and about make another buck in 10 minutes." This phone
clicking Ma" he said to Connie.
"Jus wait till the sun go down...that shit gon piss you off Papi..no
sleep . Dats da 8244 number.. I fuckin hate dat phone". Cazz said.
"Man, I'm bout to need some more grease in a second " Kills said.
"Butter got something for you" Cazz informed Kills.
"Cool"
"After dis lick you have to take me to Continental Hotel....gotta date"
Cazz said.
"Date? The fuck kinda date at the CH"? He asked confused.
"This the "Massage" phone", she said holding up a pinkish color
phone. "Its listed in the Penny saver as an erotic massage but it's
full service escort. It's like 4 other girls but they in the room waiting
on incalls.We make the trick get a room in his name and we keep it
when it's over jus go down and pay it daily. Any givin time we have
3 4 rooms in 1 or more hotels ", she explained. "We sleep in one or
two and hustle out the rest ". she explained. "That way anything
goes left we ain't got no ties to the rooms when went on.
Pulling up to the location the lick told Kills he was at, Kills notice it
was a Mercedes SL 55 in the driveway and a BMW 750LI, both
midnight black with dark tinted windows." Dis nigga gettin that fetti
my nigga",Connie said almost whispering it .
"Yea Mark a real estate agent he be getting to it Mami", Cazz
explained. "He be really off that paint though, he must need da
maximum high tonight ", she went on.
"Oh word? That nigga definitely eating ". Kills said. As the car
stopped the last person Kills thought would ever come out came
out. Light skinned wavy hair slicked back, tall well-built athletic
figure. Face was smooth except for the thin goatee he wore neatly
trimmed with a hint of grey. His strong features let you know he was
a serious man his hazel green eyes darted back in forth surveying
the street before he approached the waiting car." Hey brotha ", he
greeted Kills in an almost southern drawl, but you can tell he's been
up north a while.
"What's goody how you"? Kills asked rhetorically. "Bout to be really
good if this anything like the last time", he said excitedly handing
Kills a crispy $100 bill. "She got you my dude " Kills said motioning
to. Connie to serve the man."Got some friends coming over a little
later, gonna need a ball of soft and one of these if ya can manage
that big guy". He told Kills."Just hit the number I got you B" Kills said

14

coolly. Before speeding off he watched the man go into the house. "If these the type niggas callin I'm bout to eat like a mufucka". "Linda go to the CH in Northdale Circle" he instructed. He was about to call Papi when the phone rang again. "Yoooo " he answered knowing it was money." I need a ball my friend" a Spanish accent came through the other end." I got 280 "
"You won't get a ball but Imma bless you Pa-Pa, Nice 3 grammer "Kills promised.
"Ok Papi I in Townes and John". He said to Kills.
" Gimmie 20 minutes I'm in Northdale". Kills told the man.
"Ok Pa...I wait here". Hanging up the phone Kills said, "We gon need some more grease lemme call OG".
"What's the science big homie", Kills said after Butter answered in the 1st ring. "YG talk to me I talk back "Butter said knowing Kills was about ready to see him. "Man, you always got somn fly to say OG. But I'm almost done with this lil 3 gs I got like a grizzly left and a ball lick in da line". He explained to Butter.
"Cool sayless .Cazz wit you still"? He asked."Yea hol' on" he said handing Cazz the phone."Que Pasa Pa-Pa ?.....Ok ... Si..Si..ok Papi". She handed Kills the phone "Yooo "
"When she done with this call she gon take you Uptown to see Lex" take that bread and all the bread she got and cop an O. Then she taking you to see Nubbs", he explained the plan to Kills.
"White boy Nubbs? Doug ". He asked not sure if it's the same guy he was locked with in the county."Yea he the paint connect,well we eat together but he the nigga to see for that white girl", Butter went on.
"Oh, ok sayless B".
"Oh .. Imma need you to go get this phone from down the way B. You can hold that one too, but come see me soon as you catch that ball lick". He told Kills. "Say no more B , we pullin up to the Conti right now. She bout yo bust this move then we on the way uptown to Lex". Kills said to his big homie. "Aite see you in a minute YG".
"Ok so imma go up here so my thing and be down in like 10 15...20 at the most Pa" Cazz said grabbing her purse and reaching for the handle. "This gon be the house for a few days", she said while getting out the car. "Be right back".
She spent away walking like a runway model, her tiny waist was wrapped in a LV belt holding up her   designer jeans swaying to a beat only she heard. Her nice round behind and hips made the jeans look painted on. Her skin was like a ray of sunshine, yellow soft and bright. Long curly hair fell to the middle of her back, and

through her crop top a tattoo that was a simple butterfly with the date "11/24/01" was slightly visible. YSL frames covered her honey brown eyes as she approached the entrance of the hotel. "She kinda dope " Connie said "Ian gay but I wanna grab her booty" she confessed as if reading Kills mind. "She cool" he said nonchalantly. As they sat and waited for Cazz to return Kills thought bout his baby girl, and was about to call Sasha but decided against it, instead he called Papi ."Que pasa my friend "? He said into the phone. "Kills I see ju ready fa me Papi. I jus get some strawberry in too I'm in West Lake

Come see me" he said to Kills." Gimmie bout a hour or so Pa" Kills informed the man "Si si thas cool Papi ...jus lemme know " he told Kills. Not even 5 minutes later Cazz was exiting the Continental Hotel jus as she entered looking like a star. "See Pa-pa? Jus like dat 300", she said flashing the cash she just made."300? For what? " Connie asked inquisitively. "Shit mami this mufucka crazy ... he wants me to talk to em like a fuckin slave master while he jacks off. Ian gotta touch em nothing..jus spank em with my belt in my panties and bra. It don't take em long as you see" she said laughing and hi fiving Connie.

"Bitch I might be in the wrong game" she said to Cazz half-jokingly. "That shit crazy...But let's bust this move I need some of this cake ", Kills said telling Linda to move the car. "We goin uptown then the lick, then Butter so I can go grab this other phone from down the way. AFTER ALL THAT PAPI... I need somn to burn,", he said with a sigh." Oh I got some Piff pa ", Caz said reaching into her LV purse and pullin out a half ounce of Piff. "I need to smoke as much bullshit I got through doin this ", she explained pulling some backwoods out the purse. "Somn u need to see Papi" she said smiling.

"Ok ok mami I see you on top of shit",he said excited to smoke "Well uptown here we come" he said laughing. No sooner than he finished laughing sis the phone ring. This ring might have been the ring that made Kills fall in love with the game all over again." Yooo" He answered knowing it was cake." I need a 7 of soft and a 7 of grease "the funny voice said."And if you got any "beans" I need like 10"

Kills took the phone away from his face and all he could say was "Damn"..... he was ready to get this CAKE.....

CAKE

"The Remix"

"This shit jumpin outta control. Hurry up and Go uptown so I ca
grab this from Lex and get back to this chase".Kills said excitedly,
and not wanting the lick to call someone else. "You got it sugar "
Ms. Linda said, turning on to 680 west towards Uptown.
"Yo imma have to come see you later Pa shit clickin and I'm on this
chase".Kills hung up the phone after leaving a message on the
machine. "Traveling westbound towards Uptown Kills remembered
hearing stories bout an old man who turned $20 into 20 bricks...
"Shit sound good", he mumbled. "What sound good"? Connie
questioned." Nah ..I was thinking bout Poppa... you know that old
dude that got 20L for getting money in the 80s"? He asked.
"They said he started witta dubb of paint, cooked it up and it was
history..."Connie said ."But I think he caught a jooks or somn".
"Naw he ain't rob nobody. His daughters put em on to the Spanish
pp, his car broke down and it cost bout 200 to fix and his daughter
Cheryl I believe told em she can make 20 into 200 in a few hrs. So
she went and got a 20 of powder...this the 80s so that shit was like
93% .. cooked it up and it was the best shit. This when it first hit The
Town so they had shit on lock. Always cooked his own shit. I was
young baby but I remember Poppa" Linda explained.
"1812" Cazz told Linda as the approached the projects.
"Stay here wit Ms. Linda Imma be in and out like a bank job", he told
Connie. He followed Cazz into the dim lit, dilapidated looking
building. "Damn..that's somn you can't ever get used to", he said

waving his hand in front of his nose trying to fan the strong stench of urine away from his nostrils.

They headed towards the staircase knowing that the buildings elevators didn't wk. "What floor mami"?

"Ocho Pa" Cazz answered in a half joking manner."8th"? He asked hoping he heard wrong.

"Si 8" she said dead serious and started to ascend the stairs.

"I swear I smoke too much bud for this stair shit B" he complained trailing after her. AS they reached the 7th floor two men came out the door to their left."Daaammnn mami you pretty as hell ", one guy said.

"Gracias Papi" she said in her 1-900 voice.

"Yea talk that gwala gwala shit baby" the other guy said.

"See Pa..? This where you fucked up.Ion speak "gwala" I speak SPANISH"!! she shouted pushing pass the men.

"Fuck you ..you bean eatin bitch..." one said.

"I'll show you a bitch ", in an instant Cazz pulled a butterfly knife from her bra, and with the skill of a trained assassin and the speed of lighting she was on the man, knife to his groin and hand around his throat."Ahora me llamo otra puta te lo desafío" she said to the now terrified man. Her voice was an iced whisper. "I- I -I - I don't know what you said " the now shivering man manage.

"Call her another bitch" Kills said between laughs. He was enjoying this. " Naw I'm good mami my bad. No disrespect intended. Sorry" he pleaded the tip of the cold steal pressed against his genitals through his jeans. "Mira cómo hablas con una dama". She said .. and then she did the most unthinkable thing ever. She kisses the man's cheek and whispered "Podrías conseguir el coño", and then walked off.

"You coulda got the pussy" Kills said to the now confused man, and followed Cazz up to the 8th floor.

"Who dat"? A strong voice asked from the other side of the door.

"It's me Papi Cassandra " Cazz answered.

"Oh ok hold on ma" the voice said.

About 1 minute later the sounds of multiple locks and chains came from the metal door, before it opened. "Wassup mami my fault I was gettin dressed", the man who Kills presumed to be Lex was in his jeans and a tank top. He was a fair skinned young man, few years older than Kills. Long hair that jus sat on his head in a wild sort of way. Tattoos covered most of his torso and he was draped in gold jewelry. "So, you need a O"? He asked knowing the answer.   " Si Pa... but we got 1050 " she said.

" That's cool ma jus holla on the re, it's only 150 anyway Ian stressin it ". He explained as he went to the kitchen. "This some new shit I jus got last night". He told em as he pulled out a book bag from the oven. While he weighed out the Ounce Kills couldn't help but notice the huge scar on his back."Nigga lucky as fuck" he thought.
His thoughts were interrupted by the ringing of the cell phone.
"Yooo"
"Where you at I need it is been over 20 minutes" the voice from earlier said "I'm on my way to you now I had to go grab something else I got you" Kills informed the man.
Just as he was hanging up Lex was finished bagging up the O.
"Appreciate you big Homie will be back soon" Kills said to Lex.
"I'm Lex by the way nice to meet you" he said extending his fist.
"Kills" he bumped his fist. They left and headed back to the car. The phone rang "Yooo... yea we in the way to that ball now, but I need a 7 of that paint and like 10 beans".
"Aite jus meet me on Brookside, tell Linda take you to Jessica house ...red head Jessica.
I'll meet you there." Butter said before hanging up. "Red head Jessica's " he told Ms. Linda.
"But first lemme catch these licks", he said. As he was wrapping up the last of the licks he remembered he hadn't eating all day "I'm wild hungry" he said to no one ."Word Connie agreed.
"We stop and get somn before we get to B-side". Linda said.
After getting some Chinese food, they headed toward Jessica's which was surprisingly close.
They all filed out the car and went into the 1 family home.
"What's poppin YG"? Butter dapped Kills up and proceeded the introductions "I'm Butter " he said to Connie," This Jessie, Nubbs and Asia in the bathroom". He went on.
"Nice to me to you all ", Connie said nicely. Kills looked around the house it was actually warm and kind of homely feeling. He noticed nice lamps on each end table. Plush carpets and old cherry framed furniture. "You wanna hit this"? He heard a voice say.
He looked and noticed the plate full of cocaine on the table. "Yea I fuck around a lil bit". Kills said taking the plate and scooping the snow-white cocaine onto a credit card. "He took a sniff and instantly was taken aback by the potent drug.
"Damn that's shot some paint" Kills said taking another bump in the opposite nostril before returning the plate.
"Yea nigga that's what we sniff we give the licks the "remix" "Butter said smiling. "The remix"? Kills said feeling the effects of the drug

19

kick it."Yea nigga Nubbs mastered this shit". Butter said motioning Kills to come to the kitchen Where Nubbs was working steadily over what seemed to Kills To be endless piles of cocaine.

"Daaaaammmnnnnn that's hella paint' 'Kills said in awe.

"What up SK, Ian know you fuck wit Butter fam this my dude" Nubbs said to Kills. In county they called em SK because his last name was King."Yea man this my OG" he said to Nubbs. Nubbs was a curly Jew fro wearing husky white kid from the burbs. He lost his left ring finger in a dirt bike accident so everybody called em Nubbs."Ok " Nubbs said. "Man tell em bout the remix Nubby" Butter urged.

"What the fuck is the remix"? Kills pushed on. "When I was playing softball, we used to take creatine to build up. That shit looks Just like paint. So one day me and my boy bought some paint and asked our home girl to tell us the difference. SHE COULDNT!!The shits identical " he said excited sniffing and laughing.

"Ok"? Kills was lost.

"Ok? NIGGA WE CUT THE PAINT WITH THE CREATIN NO TASTE NO SMELL NO DIFFERENCE IN COLOR....with the quality paint I get I put 1 on 1 and get 2 . They can't tell cuz the bullshit they gettin already is not as good as the remix so they coming back' 'Butter said with the most devious smile ever.

"Nigga you look like da bad guy in every movie "Kills joked.

"Yea but unlike them I got a secret weapon that's gon make me ..naw MAKE US RICH AS FUCK...."

"Nigga what you got OG...?"

"NIGGA.THE REMIX"....

They all laughed, just as they were laughing a high-pitched voice screamed"KIIILLLLAAAAAAAAAAA"!!! Only 2 people called him that his close friend Asia Redd or the police."YOOOOO LIL SISTER WHATS POPPIN BABY"?

Kills was excited to see a good friend in such good company. "You know me sellin pussy paint and pills. P UNIT " she said laughing and bouncing her head."

I know you gettin to it sis ". Kills said proudly.

"Lemme hit somn Nubbs" Asia said. He handed her a plate from the table. "No... it's not the Remix " he assured her. "Oh, ok you know I like it raw "she said and as if on cue all four of the friends started to sing in unison "SHIMMY SHIMMY YAH SHIMMY YAH SHIMMY YAY". Kills could feel the come up.... but what goes up must come down.Or does it...but for now all he knew was he was getting to that cake and with the remix. He planned on being Diddy of the city.

CAKE

"Sleep when I'm dead"

"This been the fastest 3 weeks in my life", Kills said riding through Philly in the rented minivan.
It was Kills Butter Connie and Asia, they took a trip to The City to cop work from the new connect and ended up in Philly at the Mitchell and Ness store copping jerseys.
"Yo Butter this shit the life", Kills said over the music.
"Told you YG we gon eat baby. Like Kings" Butter said lighting a blunt.
"We ain't even start yet "Butter said between puffs. But little did they know something or someone from your past always comes back to bite you."Yo what's shaking"? Kills answers one of the 3 phones he was in control of. "Naw don't give em the remix he cheffin so jus takes it up 2 points ", he instructed.
"Ayo that was Nubbs, nigga Lex wanna cop a big 8th told em 72 flat". Kills explained. "72 ...? That bout right Butter agreed.
"Yo how you go from coppin from Lex to dropping on Lex"? Kills asked."I copped to see what HE was workin with once I knew I knew I could put em in a position to eat. And he wouldn't be able to say no. That's how a boss move YG ..put a man in position to eat ..he stay loyal" he told his younger counterparts. Kills was soaking it all up. "Damn you right ..cuz I'll die kill and go in fa you OG",He pledged.
"Asia pass da damn L ma" Butter said."Nigga I jus got it from Con",she replied lighting the Dutch. "We goin back to the city grab that from Animal and go straight home. 5 birds and 1000 pills ain't

21

somn to be riding around wit .Yall know the rules ..bogey smokin only ", He explained.

In the past 2 weeks Kills been to the City 4 times but never to grab This much weight or pills at once.

His nerves were showing after they arrived at Animal's house. "Look Pa we good you know we good we do this ", Connie said as they sat outside the building while Butter went to conduct business. After a half an hour butter came out with two books bags, and headed straight to the trunk where the rest of the luggage and shopping bags were. He purposely sat them on top. "YALL ready"? He asked not caring for answer more as to say "let's go ". They all

 Got into the van and headed back home. It was about a 3-hour ride. The girls drove most the way with either guy in the passenger seat. Just as they were entering their county state troopers got behind them. "OH my God oh my God Oh my God "!!!! Connie said. "Troopers behind us." She told the car.

"So? You got Ls ya car legal fuck em ". Butter said. As if to say "challenge accepted, the highway patrol car's lights lit up the night sky like Independence Day fireworks. "These fuckin crackers ain't got shit better to do", complained, Butter from the passenger seat. "Everybody chill and jus shut up", he instructed. Connie was visibly nervous. "Mami relax, you good he can't search without a warrant ya permission or probable cause. The car clean and legal jus like you". He said with confidence. "Good evening ma'am License and registration please", the officer said.

"Hey officer you mind me explaining why we're being pulled over "? Butter asked from his seat."

"I'll explain to the driver in a minute. Now ma'am if you would be so kind as to hand me your license and registration. Please " he repeated. " I-I I lost my wallet ", she said damn near in tears. Butter felt his heart drop in his chest.

"Well lemme have ya registration please ma'am and your full name and date of birth "he said to Connie who was all but shaking now, she told the officer her information.

"Ok ma'am I'll be back shortly, would ya mind turning your vehicle off for me please ", the cop requested. Connie complied and turned the car off.

"Tell me you got Ls ma...like dead ass if you don't you taking the wrap". Butter said through clenched teeth. Connie was silent she personally didn't have license but she often used her older sister who lived in Arizona info and got away with it. " Ma'am can you step out the car for me please,"? He asked her. "For what... what she

22

does?" Kills asked aggravated." Sir please calm down" I'll explain everything when I'm done., but for now please keep calm and stay in the van".

"This some bullshit", Asia said, she had a bench warrant for missing court so she kept her comments to a minimum. "Kills I hope ya girl don't fold B", Butter said in a low voice," I really hope she solid, I like her, but my FREEDOM somn I LOVE", he told em looking through the review. It seemed like an eternity before the cop returned." She has givin me consent to search the vehicle I'm gonna need y'all to step out please," he informed the rest of the crew. At this point Kills was ready to grab the work and run, only problem was he had no idea where he was. "Officer we have a deadline to meet sir with all so respect this is some bull" Kills said exiting the van as he did so another trooper pulled up.

Black serious looking man. You can tell he took his job waaaaayyyy to serious. "Y'all jus stand by while I take a look inside", the first officer said. As they watched him go through the front of the car their hope begins to leave. As he approached the truck he said "Anything back here I should know about "? "I have a bottle of Hennessy opened but it was before we got on the road and I'm not driving", Kills said hoping his honesty helped out a little bit, or maybe even throw the officer off." That's fine sir I appreciate the honesty ", the officer told Kills.

He then grabbed the two book bags with the drugs in it, "Whose are these "? He asked, before anyone could say something Kills said "Mines sir". Butter looked at him flabbergasted. He couldn't believe the younger man would stand tall even if it wasn't his.

The officer opened one of the bags and said "Jackson, cmere". As the other officer walked towards the back of the van Kills body went limp. He was 22 and he knew he wasn't coming home for at least 15. 20 years. " Sir can you come here please", the officer who pulled em over motioned for Kills to come over to him. Kills mustard up the strength and walked to the front of the car." Ok this can go 1 of 2 ways" the officer began." "1 you can stick to ya story, I take you to county go through all the motions you get convicted and get 30 years for trafficking with intent to distribute. Or you can be honest and tell me who this really belongs to. Your choice your life", he told Kills. Without hesitation Kills said" I'm not a felon and I've never been arrested, I might get 15. I'll do about 7, come home and be a free man. So, like I said it's mines so take me in and let my friends go, that ain't even know I had that in the car", Kill went on."Ok have your way", the officer started to cuff Kills when he heard Butters voice say "Aite man that's enough ,I can't take no more", all while laughing hysterically. "Wait... what fuck goin in"? kills said in total confusion.

"This my cousin and his partner " Butter started, "The streets is so fucked up ya right hand gotta hide from ya left... Niggas will ride when the money flowing. but when the shit hit the fan....niggas sit on the stand. But YOU... YOU? You a different breed YG ..I had to make sure you wasn't a nigga who would fold under pressure. And you didn't, I know you would hold it down you were ready to go up north for me, THATS the kinda nigga I need as at side". Butter said with passion.

"Nigga you coula had me pop a nigga, rob a Papi, hell you coulda made me take a blood oath, but you have us pulled and the police find da work "? Kills said still not believing what was going on.

"Man, I need a fuckin blunt NOW"!!! Kills said walking back in forth trying to wrap his finger around the situation. "So, what's good wit Connie"? He asked s concerned." When I pulled her out I told her what was goin on, surprisingly she was saying NOTHING even after I told her the scoop ", the officer said laughing and lighting a cigarette " Butter this might be the team you need lil cuz " Jackson said. Asia was just sitting there stuck. She was so nervous she still hadn't realized it was all a test."Lemme let her out the car I'm sure she curious as to what's happening ", the cop said." You did great YG, this won't go unnoticed, hear me"? Butter grabbed Kills up and hugged the man like his son" You different

YG the game need more niggas like you", he said and walked to the police car. "Follow me for the next hour,I got somn for y'all" He told his cousin. " No doubt cutty,but on grams, he a solid lil nigga ,keep em".

" I am ...I am".

"Aite lets go yall this cake waiting, "Butter said gettin in the driver seat."Kills up front YG. We good money till the Town". Kills got in the front and started cracking a Dutch." I can't front ...I was wild petro ", he confessed. "But I wasn't saying shit but what I did already", he continued." Man, that nigga said it was a test, I was thinking he tryna get me to eat" Connie said. "Bitch bye ain't no snitch in my blood, straight jacket " she said also cracking a blunt." Yall held it down, and for that my gratitude will be shown", Butter promised. For the next several miles they rode in silence. When they finally reached the Town, the girls were sleep and Kills was rolling another blunt,"YG", Butter began "You did exactly what I needed you to do. You claimed ya shit", he said. "What? Mines?

Nigga this ya work", Kills said half joking. Naw YG we made this trip
fa you. What you think imma be feeding you and you got the tools to
go eat? Naw a real nigga doesn't feed his brother THEY EAT
TOGETHER. Cazz ain't stay cuz the
Penny saver ..or to catch licks.. My Papi was dropping of 10 of them
thangs for me. I'm good YG, but now WE good", he said to his little
partner. "Butter...I really don't know what to say OG..I'm stuck ", he
said his mind blown. 1000 pills and 5 birds. "Man, all you gotta Do is
answer ya phone, the money gon flow. You earned this, ya loyalty
was proven", he said to Kills. As they were pulling up to the
Continental Hotel Kills asked "What if I woulda snitched "? I'm jus
sayin hypothetically speakin of course".
"Well ... that 30 he told you bout? You woulda had to hold that
down. Soon as you flipped they woulda took us all, we woulda been
ok, you...well lets jus say ,my cousin woulda painted the picture so
good ..you woulda been buried under the jail". Butter said his eyes
were cold as a polar Bears toenails." Good thing I'm a G", Kills said
trying to lighten the mood." Yea good thing ", Butter said. "But real
shit Ian gon be able to get NOOOOO sleep now" Kills half
complained .Butters looked at his protégé and said "They print
money while we sleep ..Ian been to sleep in years...I'll sleep when
I'm dead"

CAKE

" NUTSO"

"Yoooo" Kills answered the phone while turning into the parking lot
of an apartment building.
"Where you at B"? The voice questioned eagerly. "OH, shit
Nutso...my bad g where you bro"? Kills asked remembering Nutso
was comin up from Albany projects in Brooklyn."Nigga I'm at the bus
station, dirty as a motherfucker."

"Fuck!!! You got here fast as fuck G... I'm in East Village dropping somn off", Kills explained trying to think of how he was going to get Nutso to a safe house." What's the addy to da spot"? Nutso asked anxious to get somewhere safe.

"Just go to the Marionette on Townsend 5210. " Kills instructed not knowing how he planned to get there. "Aite I'm on my way B" Nutso told him while flagging a taxi.

"If you beat me there jus tell Connie or Cazz what the deal is .any issues call me ",Kills instructed.

"Mother fuckin Nutso" Kills said aloud while steering the A6 Audi he just copped a week before. Pearl white it came down the ave lookin like a cloud of smoke.

On the way from his drop and heading towards the marionette to meet Nutso, he recalled the first time they met.

"AYO this my phone B .. ion give a fuck what nigga say or think ..I'm from Brooklyn". The short slightly fat dark-skinned man shouted in a raspy voice." Real shit b, niggas gotta problem they can play the cell " he continued. Kills was playing chess with his homie Boogie. "This nigga bugging, I use whatever phone I want" Boogie said loud enough so the pod could hear. "Chill B ...son gon don't know how we rock " Kills said moving a knight. "Checkmate".

"Man that's some Bull shit .." Boogie complained. "I'm bout to go play ball " he said before heading to the gym. Shortly after Nutso entered the gym. "Aye now what you were sayin bout MY phone "? He asked Boogie." Nigga we got rules and order here and THAT phone the open phone. Everybody use it. Now ion know what you rep or where you from but niggas got phones. You said BK ok the Red Hook niggas got the 3rd phone " Boogie explained not really wanting a problem but ready for whatever.

"Naw homie that phone ..MINES ..when I wanna use it no matter who on it I'm gon use it ..dig me" ? He said walking towards Boogie. "My g that ain't what we doin is it"? Kills said entering the gym. "It's not ya business what I'm doin" Nutso said. His eyes were iced. Nutso walked wit a limp being he was shot over 11 times. He used to say "Nigga I'm bullet proof" Growing up in Albany projects wasn't an easy thing. He was walking towards Kills and just stopped mid stride "where you from " he asked, the question threw both Kills and Boogie off.

"Why"? Kills asked ready for action if needed."Cuz you look like my man Smoke P people" he replied looking more closely at Kills features. Kills was 6'2 165 dark. Not very dark more like chocolate. Slender athletic build, short hair and medium brown eyes. "Smoke my lil cousin. How you know him"? He asked now even more on point.

"You used to be at his house in Harlem in Wagner. We used to ball at 45. I was skinny back then, you used to come every summer". Nutso said reminding Kills about his childhood days. "Yoooo this fuckin crazy B" Kills said remembering the boy."Man shit was bout to get ugly in this bitch" Kills said laughing.

"Son y'all niggas know each other "? Boogie said extremely confused at what just happened. "Yea man for a lil minute too"Nutso said. "So, what's the jack niggas be using Sha"? He called Kills by his nickname." Niggas call me SK now, what they call you Kev"? He asked Nutso.

"Shell" he said.

" "Shell" "? Kills asked?

"Yea nigga, like crazy, shell shocked", he explained.

That shit nuts my dude" Boogie said laughing. From then on it was Nuts or Nutso.

Kills pulled up not long after the yellow taxi dropped Nutso off.

"Yooo my motherfuckin Nigga Shell"!! He said laughing loudly.

"Sha-Sha ..black fucker" he replied embracing his old friend. " Fuck you fat boy" Kills shot back.

"Nigga I was jus bout to call yo ass man ". He told Kills reaching for the duffel bag he brought with him.

"The fuck your got in their nigga"? Kills asked pointing to the bag.

"The machine nigga", he said in a low voice. He followed Kills into the apartment, locked the door and headed straight to the kitchen.

"Nigga what THE FUCK IS THAT"!!! Kills said lookin at Nutso pull the gun out the bag. "Tech nigga" he said putting the clip into the gun. " that bitch look like somn from terminator. She got air holes and shit",he said like a small child admiring a new toy . " Nigga I gotta shoot this shit ", Kills said reaching for the weapon." Not now nigga later", Nutso told Kills putting the weapon on top of the table.

"Ok ok ok . But soon as the sun down I'm lettin that thang off" he said eyeing the death machine.

"Yea aite my g but first roll somn up nigga .I been on that bus for 5 hours no smoke witta tech. A nigga nerves shot",Nutso said " Look in da cabinet above the stove it's some Piff up dere B". While Nutso rolled a blunt Kills called Connie.

"What's good PA"? She answered her phone on the 1st ring." Where you at "? He asked.

"Date".

"Ok mami come to the M when you finish", he instructed.

"Ever since Asia been around Connie been working with her at China Dolls.

"Bitch you be fuckin and suckin for free or for problems. Might as well get that bread. Most these niggas last 5 minutes max. Or they wanna see you dance in ya panties and bra bitch", Kills hears Asia talking to Connie a week or so ago." Ion know ma, I mean it seems easy but I jus can't see myself doin that wit a stranger. Especially an old white dude". Connie said.

"Like I said mami free fuckin ain't where it's at. Cake baby that's what's it's bout. Look I got a date that want 2 girls to dance and make out in somn sexy .350 a piece 30 minutes. He probably gon jerk off and cum in 5, if he does then we out in 5 bitch". Asia said laughing and hi fiving Connie.

"Aite Asia I trust you bitch Imma come and do it but first I need a bean" she said referring to an Ex pill. They been selling and popping E more frequently now that they had a bigger flow thanks to Asia. Asia been in the streets since she was 14. She was always pretty. Light skinned with slightly slanted eyes that were a glowing greenish grey. Long curly hair she always had done or in a neat bun. Her face was almond shaped and flawless with the exception of a small scar on her left side of her lip, where she fell on her skates as a child. Her body developed earlier than most children her age. At 11 she had the body of most 16 or 17-year olds. Her step father was a drunk abusive man who used to watch her while she bathed. He never touched her just seemed to always be around when she showered or bathed. She tried to tell her mother who also was an alcoholic and a coke addict, but always got beat and accused of being fast. One day a few days after her 14th bday she was awakened by a moaning sound. She was used to hearing her mother and step father having sex through the paper-thin walls, but this was closer than normal. This seemed to be coming from the room. She opened her eyes to see her step father standing over her master-bating. She jumped up and ran to her mother's room, only to find her passed out drunk. "She no help to ya lil perrty ass now", he slurred.

She ran into the kitchen with him following pants down yelling "YOU WANNA BE GROWN!! ILL MAKE YOU FEEL LIKE A REAL WOMAN"!!

"Leave me alone Jake ", she said backing up against the fridge.
"Cmere honey,lemme kiss you", he reached out and grabbed her by
the hair. In that moment, she felt his hot beer and menthol breath on
her face. She reached out to fight him but he was too strong as he
forced his body against hers.
Asia reached to her left and felt a pan. She lifted the pan and swung
with everything she could.
PING!!!! The cast iron struck his head with the force of a bowling
ball full speed, instantly opening his scalp exposing the skull. The
sound of his skull cracking was sickening, almost like cracking crab
legs. He fell to the floor unconscious. Asia didn't stay to see if he
ever woke up She packed her bag took the pan and left. Never to
return. That was 3 years ago. Since then she has been in shelters
hotels and friend's couches. Then she met Dom. He put her into the
escort game and it was like she found her calling. She made money
traveled and partied like a rock star. She met Kills when she was
15. They were at a hotel and she was fighting with a trick who didn't
want to pay. Kills helped her get her money and they were tight ever
since.
"Man, you still can't roll nigga". Kills said entering the kitchen and
looking at the blunt Nutso rolled.
"Nigga I taught you how to roll member that ", he said looking for a
lighter." True story ", Kills agreed. "But what you doin up here, what
you got goin on B"?
"Naw I jus was locked up and I need a come up. You know I be on
my BK bs. S.U.K stick up kid " he said puffing the L.
" It's a few niggas Imma jooks". He said rubbing his hands together.

"First stop West side. Gotta get a few Papis . I know they ready fa
me". He said knowing that's an easy jooks. "Just be careful out here
nigga. They playing da keeps. Lil niggas too. That's who wildin out
here ". Kills cautioned his child hood friend." First off .. hit this
ma'fuckin Piff . Second ion give a flyin fuck bout no lil nigga, . And
third. when this machine get in they face all that gangsta shit
disappear . Lastly ... nigga IM MOTHER FUCKIN NUTSO"!!!!

CAKE

29

"I can feel it in the air"

"Ok Papi ...put ya fuckin hands on the wall. Your fuckin move. imma shoot you in ya fuckin face". The masked man said. The man was short and had a skinny frame, and a high-pitched voice.
 "Where it at? I know you got it Papi so let's not play" the bigger guy said. " I need all da Piff ..."he had a .38 special aimed at his head.
"Nada pa-pa nada" he said in Spanish.
"You think it's a game? Nigga I'm not playin", he said spinning the man around and cocking the hammer on the pistol.
"First ..lemme get them chains and ya watch and ya bracelet AAAANNNDDD ya rings too. Second my lil man bouta tear this shit up fa that fetti ,and that work. So y'all sit tight and if we find it before y'all tell us... muerto ", he said using his thumb to symbolize death by a cutting of the throat motion.
"AYO tear this mother up B" he instructed. 10 minutes later the smaller man returned wit 5 pounds of weed and more jewelry.
"We good B ", the man told his partner. "Let's dip".
"Naaaaawwww man", he told the man. "We ain't get no bread, Papi playing. Nigga where the fuckin money"? he asked removing a box cutter from his champion hoody.
He places the cold rusty metal against the man's cheek and slowly slid the razor-sharp blade downward, cutting deep into the man's flesh."AARRRRGGGHHHH"!!!!!! The man's screams were agonizing and pierced the air like a archers arrow.
"Yeeeeeaaaaa ... you wanna b Tony Mon-fuckin-tana right Papi? Well here's a scare face puta", he said
"Now unless you want ya pretty lil girl to get her food ate so y'all can have matching scars ... tell me where that money at"!!!
Before the man could answer they lady screamed "IN THE FLOOR ..ITS IN THE FLOOR IN THE BACK BEDROOM DOWNSTAIRS"!!!!
She began to sob uncontrollably.
"Mucho gracias Miami", the robber said with a chuckle." See pa it coulda been easy...reeeeeaaalllll fuckin easy but nope .. You Tony .. now you look like em "., he said before tying the man up.

"Get that and we out ", he told the other robber. He went to the room where the lady victim said he would find the money. "JAAAACCKKKKPOT"!!!!!!
"Papi you was eatin huh", the man said coming out holding a large hockey bag with what had to be at least 50k in cash. "You was holding out huh pa"? The large man asked. The bag had 9 ounces of heroine, 3 kilos of coke and 3 lbs. of some weed they never saw.

"Yea we goody baby, we out .Thanks for the donation my friend ". He said in a terrible Spanish accent. The men ran two blocks north to the awaiting getaway car they parked earlier.
"Niiigggaaaa this was the one Wease", Nutso said removing his mask and starting up the car. "Word big bro, this was a power Jooks", the man Nutso called "Wease" said in agreement.
"Papi had 4 Cubans, 2 with the Jesus pieces like 2 bracelets a few rings-iced out too,...man he was gettin it B", Wease went on taking inventory as Nutso steered the car to the safe house.
"I'm bout hit up all da big-time niggas and get all them jewels off", Nutso said already knowing Kills And his man P Grams was gon want em all probably.
"We good for a minute. We gon sit in that paper, and sell all the work wholesale. So naw we ain't got nothin less than a big 8th", he explained the plan to Wease. 4.5 ounces of coke was a big 8th or an 8th of a kilo. Kilos was going for 18k -22.5k. At 18 you had to know somebody. Kills was getting for 18. 500 a zip he said straight down." If this coke some paint ... we dropping it's for 19-5   All day . If it's stepped on or not super fire 17-5., feel me"?
" Most def. but I got a few peoples in da Capital thata pay 25, and better for it. Man, truth be told I rather take that lil 2-hour trip and eat lovely. Plus, I know that boy gon love it at a crazy number on the hood", Wease countered the plan with an alternate one.
"Lil bro ...less is more. Less risk more security. We pop up in da Capital wit allllll this work, for da low. What you think type attention we gon draw? Jack boys like us and police ass niggas. Man, ion know bout you Wease but I'm good on em both ", Nutso told his young partner. " We can make a killing though B", he said sounding disappointed.
"Tell you what" ,Nutso started "You take ya half and do what you wan do lil bro", he proposed.
"Man Imma show you what I mean big bro. Watch how I come back all chipped up", he said laughing.

The men pulled into the apartment building lot and started to gather the take from the heist they just had pulled.

"Now .. you hit it wit the ice, and watch that shit lock like white people car doors when a nigga walks by", Kills said to Connie. He was teaching her how to cook coke into crack. "Yeeeaaahhh baby yeeeeeaaahhhhh...look at dat ting get busy ", he said excitedly.

"Yoooo ". He answers his phone.

"What up brother"? the voice on the other end greeted.

"Juuuuiicceee , what's good bro"? Kills asked instantly recognizing the voice as his brother Juice.

They were actually 1st cousins but they were so close it was more like siblings." Ain't shit bro tryna get that north side money", Juice said.

"I'll be down the way in a minute bro we gon chop it up", Kills told em. "Aite I'm at Max crib bro you know it's the 1st need all this ", Juice said to Kills.

"Say no more big bro ,gimme an hour or 2".

"Nigga day mean 3 or 4", Juice replied jokingly.

" Naw we gotta bust a move on Dolvin and Topside anyway ", Kills told him.

"Cool we here".

"That's the last O in that bird, you want me to bust a new o e open "? Connie was standing in the kitchen   an empty turkey bag that once had a kilo of cocaine.

"Naw we good, Nutso bout to bring me 2 joints .I wanna see what they cook like", he explained after seeing a text from Nutso."2 joints for 18 a pop .... jus left Papi

"Nutso"? She asked. "What niggas he jooksed "? She asked knowing it didn't matter.

"Papi" he answered.

"Damn he be wilding ".

" We hustle dope pills pussy crack whatever..and Nutso and Wease rob niggas, better to have em on This side ma", he said walking to the kitchen.

"Put this shit in a bag and weight it up in O's. Set 4 and half out ", he instructed. " I gotta go meet Butter".

"No problem Pa. Who them 4 for"? She asked.

"Hi Face", it's on the arm so he good I'm gon send em over in like a hour. Jus meet em by the Citgo on 7th North, take the Beamer", he told her .

"Aite pa, I got you ".

He grabbed a quarter of Piff and slid out the door.
He was driving down the street when his private line rang.
" Hello"?
"Hurry up YG", Butter voice seemed a little strained.
"I'm on Allen pullin up in like 3 minutes. You good OG"?
"Yea YG ... I'm good", he answers sounding a little uneasy.
"Ok .. I'm in route "
He hung up wondering what could be the problem. He detected
something he just couldn't put his finger on it.
"I know my OG", he whispered as he pulled into Butters 4-bedroom
5 bath homes driveway.
"What's good YG? You got them joints fa me"? Butter didn't even
give him time to get out the car.
"Naw .. I wa-"
"Damn YG!!! I told you bring me 3 kilos of coke "He said loudly.
" Damn OG chill you makin a movie B", Kills said confused on why
he spoke like that.
"Man, I need to make this move really quick" he said walking
towards the garage.
"Imma holla at you Shaquille ", he said,disappearing from view into
the 3 car garage.
"Somn ain't kosher", Kills mumbled before taking off.
"Juice I'm 5 minutes away bro".
"Hurry up this shit jumping" he said .Kills made a left on to Dolvin ,"
I'm on Dolvin now ", he told Juice.
A minute later he was parking his 750 LI in front of his cousin's
house. "Ok lil bro. da 50 look real nice on them Lexanis" Juice said.

"Man, this light...wait till I bring that G wagon out this summer", he
said hugging his brother.
"SKKIIII RRROOOOCCCCCKKKKKK!!!!!! WHERE DAY AT"? a
voice called from behind Juice. It was his older cousin /brother Dead
Arm.
"What up brother"? Dead Arm or D.A asked? "Shit bout to take
Juice to bust a move, you riding"? " Naw my lil bitch coming
through. And its da 1st I'm out here ya heard? But I see you gettin
all the money nigga. Beamer 3 phones on ya neck", he said
reaching for a phone." "Pimp Stress"? The fuck you got poppin
Kills"? He said reading the captions on one of Kills phones.
"Pimpin ain't easy baby", he replied like an old school Pimp.
They all laughed and smoked a brunt before Kills said "You ready? I
hit wild shit to do".

"Yea c'mon. Let's slide'" Juice said.

The jumped in the luxurious car and heard to the north.

"Yo what's shakin big bro "? Kills asked over the Dip Set music playing.

"Man, I need one of these joints lol bro. For real", Juice replied.

"Fuck wit me and you gon have a Few joints ". He promised. They pulled up to the spot and Soon as they got out the car, Nutso pulled up behind them.

" Nuuuutttssssooo... what's the word "? Kills said excited knowing his old friend had something for them.

"Bird. That's the word 2 of them thanks. Couple Cubans and some dog food", he said hold in up a back pack."Damn nigga "!!! Kills and Juice said at the same time.

"Let me get in this house sink can see what yo ass done got " Kills said leading them men upstairs .

"Juice .. grab that bag out the trunk".

After the men all got inside Kills locked the door and directed the men to the kitchen. "Now lemme see what them pies lookin like baby", he said rubbing his hands together, wearing a sinister grin. Nutso begin to unload the bag.

"That shit is crazy my guy", juice said picking up a custom Cuban chain with an iced-out Jesus piece. The chain was diamond encrusted and at least 36 " long. The pendent was incredibly covered in VVS diamonds and the eyes were 2 carat red rubies, that match the crown of thorns.

"Yea this shit is like dat my nigga", Nutso replied continuing to take items out of the bag.

" That chain definitely sold my g", Kills said taking the chain from Juice and putting it around his neck. "You can get the other one though". He said referring to a slightly shorter chain with no charm.

"Nigga hell yea", Juice said putting his new jewelry on.

"Now back to these things. let's dance" Kills said taking the cocaine

to the stove and preparing to cook it into crack. At that moment Connie came in the kitchen.

"Hello gentlemen ", she said in Nutso and Juice direction.

"Hi came and grabbed dat. Butter called me and said you said put three whole up for em. I told I was gon call when you got here. Nigga gave me a weird vibe Pa. Before you go in I know he ya mans ...BUT he was wild hot on the jack. He said ya government and said "kilos of coke". I was like ... nah this seems crazy", she said with a look in concern on her face.

34

"Open that bag up", Kills said.

When she opened the bag, it was 3 Kilos of cocaine, neatly wrapped.

They all looked at each other.

"So why you ain't give em the work you said you was meeting em", she asked.

"Same reason you ain't give it to em ... I felt that same shit you did ma. Somn ain't kosher ", he said in a low voice. As if it was a secret code the men started grabbing all the product and put them into bags.

"We goin to my house", Kills said.

"Ya house HOUSE"? Connie asked baffled.

"Yea Butter never came there. We always go to the spots or his lil butch crib. Connie take the work and go to ya house and meet me at mines. Don't take ya Lex ...take ya Honda ma . Low key", he said in nearly a whisper. They all headed down stairs quietly, as if they were teenagers sneaking out the house
on a school night.

"Straight there and to my crib". He said firmly. "Nutso ride wit me real quick. I got some bread at the house. I got you."

"Say no more ,lemme move the v", Nutso replied .Kills got into a Dodge Caravan he rented a week earlier. The other 2 followed shortly. "I can't trust nobody he introduced me to,", Kills said aloud.

" Yo what the fuck goin on"? Juices asked paranoid.

"I think this nigga Butter tryna set me up B", Kills answered in a low voice. "NIGGA WHAT"? Both men said simultaneously. " Yea man he been actin funny the last few weeks but I thought it was a bitch or somn .But now I'm thinkin he been coming to get weight from the spot way more than normal. But I'm thinking a few zips here and there ain't nothing serious. Though he got some hoes party ..or a sample ...hell even him puttin a nigga on like he did me", He explained. "But how you know this nigga Sha", Nutso asked. "From back in da days he always was ah ol' head I looked up too hot lonely looked out type shit", he explained. Then he told them about the time he saw him in the pjs.

"Man, this shit sound like a fuckin movie G. Or a Donald Goines joint" Nutso said shaking his head.

"I gotta act like Ion know nothin cuz , I gotta figure out what he doin".

"Bro, he Trina get you booked", Juice said, cracking s Dutch.

"Why I don't know. but this obvious".

"Hello ..." Kills phone answered the phone.

"I'll accept " He said.
"Papi ... get me out. My bail 10 gs ...or 1k with bondsman" Asia said quickly, her voice firm.
"Freeze pops"? He asked
"No, popsicles", she said flatly.
"Con ed gon put the lights back on". He hung up the phone.
"Asia booked on some soliciting shit her bail a G" he was on another call."When you done meet me at the bat cave" he said to Connie.
"Say no more pa on it" Connie replied. The call ended.
"This shit crazy...", Kills said to no one In particular.
"Yea you need this ", Juice said passing the L. "Yo... why me Though? He was the man.... he put me on. Somn ain't right b... I can feel it in the air".... Kills said.
"Yoooo ...... WHAT?!! NAH!! WHAT HOSPITAL"??!! Nutso voice was a cracked whisper.... the phone dropped from his grasp and he headed for the door. The air don't lie.... Kills thought... " I can feel it....in the air"... Beenie lyrics played in his head as he headed out behind Nutso.

CAKE

"ALL GOOD THINGS"

  "I kept my end of the bargain. Where the honor in ya word".?
Butter sat in the CID part of the precinct talking to the Federal agents and the Drug task force captain.
"Bradford, we do have your boy in custody ..convicted and serving time. Yea you got me a big case, and it will help clean up the city. But I can't just let you off. It's trafficking with intention to distribute over 50 kilos of cocaine", the agent said.
"We've been doin this dance for over a year now. You're just getting me a solid lead on a big case. Your tapes and phone conversations will get him 5 years maximum for conspiracy. The footage on the

highway it's a good start. But you didn't get him buying or having it in his possession", the other officer added.

"He admitted it was his", Butter pleaded his case. He was facing life without parole if convicted. He was not ready for that. He'd become an accustom to the lifestyle. But he was in a position that he couldn't afford to deal with.

"Look I know you got something for me Brad. Someone...." that's the first time he had ever had a federal agent interrogating him. He was shaking up.

"I know a few guys selling weed, out west", he said hoping that was enough.

"I hope it's a fucking farm full" the agent said sarcastically." I need coke crack guns or heroine. You got caught with 50 kilos.50 FUCKING KILOS .. I don't know why I'm even trying to strike a deal.".

"Ok ...I'll get you what you need . You have anybody in mind"?
He wasn't trying to give up his plug hoping he could still do business after all this passed.

"How about Rod? He's been moving major weight on the East for a while now. We can't ever get anything solid to stick".

"I can do it like third party style"? He asked the agent not wanting to compromise his credit in the streets.

"I don't care how you do it get 4 kilos from em" the officer knew the man copped a lot more than that and it would look suspect for him to only cop 4, but he didn't care at all about that, he wanted to get Rod. That was 3 years ago. Butter has been setting up Kingpins and big-time drug dealers for the FBI they didn't know he was making the men overnight. After all his close friends were set up by him and a few connects out of town, his wire was running thin. He needed someone running an elaborate operation. When he saw the young man, he used to give dollars and bags of weed, he knew he would be able to make him bigger than life. Not a real handsome man so the woman wouldn't be a distraction he thought as the young man approached him.

The others weren't enough they said. 2 connects beat the cases on technicalities and received minimum sentences. The others were only buy and bust and a few kilos. He had to figure it out fast or he was getting the minimum of 20 that's with his cooperation. Butter wasn't a prison built guy, mentally.

Paroled after 10, he couldn't see himself in that place for that long.

"I'm gon get you somn ...jus have my pardon ready". Butter coming to. "48 hours Brad...48" the agent said walking away.

Butter left the precinct feeling paranoid and pressured. He knew the young boy was very smart and attentive so his recent actions were sure to tip him off, if not already.

"Damn..voicemail again", he said aloud. After dialing Kills number for a 3rd time in a row.

"Aye man what the fuck is goin on B"! Kills screamed running after Nutso out of the front door.

"Niggas shot Wease OT!!! He in critical. I gotta get there yo.. "he answers fumbling for his keys.

"What the fuck!!!! Naw bro ...naw ...we was just wit em," Kills said feeling his soul leave his body.

"Dem Capital niggas hit eem up. I swear imma kill em all B", Nutso promised starting the car up.

"Ayo want me come wit you"? Kills asked opening the car door.

"Naw... go take care that funny shit B I be back in a few days. Hold dat choppy fa me too", he said pulling off. Kills mind shifted back to Butter this wasn't sitting right with him. "Connie go get Asia NOW"! Kills said motioning Connie towards the other vehicle.

Kills and Juice jumped in his ride and proceeded to go meet Butter.

"Man, I hope da lil nigga aite B" Juice said lighting a Dutch.

"Put that out bro we dirty as fuck," Kills said after smelling the pungent aroma of the marijuana.

They rode all the way to the south side in silence, Kills mind racing a mile a minute.

"Yo,my bad OG niggas   wildin, I'll put you on when we link." Kills said into his cell.

"Damn YG everything cool"? Butter asked calmly?

"Yea, like I said, in person. Meet me in the Pjs. He said before hanging up not waiting for Butter response.

"Look bro Imma drop you off if I need you be on standby. I don't want this comin back on you. Take this phone call Connie and yall link wit Cazz after she gets Asia. She knows where to go." Kills instructed Juice handing him phone.

He dropped Juice off and went to meet Butter. He didn't have the 3 kilos on him, Kills was too smart for that. "Possession is 9/10 of the law "he said quietly to self. He pulled up to the store in his Pjs and parked on the side. "Big money "!

Kills heard a voice from across the street. "Saaaabbbb"... what's goody my dude "? Kills greeted his old friend Saab in the middle of the street with a hug.

"Nothin man fresh out ...got caught up in some bullshit fuckin wit Rod ", he began as they walked toward the store. "Wooorrrdd damn

Ian know you got caught up in that shit in the Valley" Kills said remembering hearing about a big raid in the Valley a few years back.

"Yea man ...matter fact you member that nigga that used to give us lil few dollars when we was lil niggas? The older fly nigga ...dark skinned chipmunk face dude."? He said to Kills trying to jar the name out his memory bank.

Kills heart dropped. He knew it was Butter but waited and played confused at Saab.

"Man, it was wild OGs back then who looked out. But what hap-" before Kills could finish a sentence a small gray Mercedes-Benz CLS stopped at the corner and roll the window down. A Puerto Rican man stared at Kills with the look that could freeze a man's soul.

"Que pasa Pa"? Kills asked irritated he was being grilled.

The man just rolled up the window and pulled off slowly.

"But anyway, my g ... what you was saying again" Kills continued trying to get Saab back into the story."

''Oh, yea anyway oh boy was supposed to had set Rod up. Nigga put em in the loop on some humbug shit, Rod got his bread up and was eating for a minute .I ran into em he hit me wit a lil elbow of some haze you know i dont fuck wit nuthin else boy. But I came to re and niggas raided the spot. Wild hammers, weight and pills." He said describing the raid in great detail. Kills body went numb after he heard the first part of what Saab said. He wasn't even listening to anything else he was saying after that, all he could think of was "oh boy put him in the loop on some humbug shit". That sentence kept playing in his head.

"But yea my g watch that nigga man he ain-... AYO ain't that the same car my g" he stops and switched subject mid-sentence after noticing the Benz riding by again, this time it didn't stop.

"Niggas don't want no static" Kills said snapping back into the moment.

"Nigga that chain is wicked "!!!! Saab said grabbing the Jesus piece he just got from Nutso.

"It's a lil somn." Kills said laughing it off. Trying to be cool.

" I'm bout to get low I'll meet you at my building put your number in my phone link up" Saab said handing Kills his phone. The old friends shook hands and parted ways. Kills mind race a million miles a minute. He couldn't believe the information he just heard about his OG. "This can't be life," he said to himself. Just then his thoughts were interrupted a voice.

"Mr. King" the voice was so familiar yet he never heard it.
"And you are "? Kills asked the obvious detective in the cheap suit.
"I'm Agent Quatrone and this is my partner Lursh, you got a minute
"? The agent asked.
"Naw I don't I'm jus leaving actually", he answered dryly and started
to walk to his car. "But you haven't seen Butter yet", the other agent
said. Kills froze unintentionally. "Yea we know everything. So let's
have a chat Mr.Ki-" his words were cut off by the loud sounds of
machine guns. BBBDDDDDDD-BBBBDDDDDDD
BBBBDDDDDDD!!! The machine sounded like a drum roll from the
war drums of Olympus. Another series of rapid fire followed. The
agents were riddled with bullets. Kills ran for cover. He dove behind
the gate by the dumpster as he felt the sharp, burning sensation of
 bullets hitting his chest arm and legs.
He was in and out of consciousness when he felt the tugging of the
Cuban chain he had on. Then all went black.

"I swear imma kill em all lil bro" Nutso said to the air. Wease didn't
make it. He had internal bleeding in his lungs. They couldn't save
him. Nutso received the call 10mins ago. Now he was riding around
the Capital with a tech 9 and fire in his eyes. "Idgaf who everybody
dyin" he continued to speak to himself. He came up on Maple Ave a
notorious street known for drug trafficking, prostitution and
 gangbanging. As usual on a Friday night the streets were littered
with crackheads, crack, dealers and prostitutes. The news reported
this where the shooting took place, so Nutso knew someone out
here knew something of Wease's death. He parked his car on the
opposite side of the street where most of the dealers were hanging
out. He jumped out machine in hand and walk hastily towards the
crowded corner of Maple and Pond. Before he reached the corner,
he raised the machine and began to spray up the whole block. The
rapid fire ripped through street signs, windows, and cars. He was
sparing no one. After the 50 shots in his original clip was emptied he
reloaded with a 30 shot clips and continue shooting everything and
anyone in sight. He then ran to his car and pulled off. After the
gunfire 7 laid dead and over 20 more were injured. A complete
blood baths. Nutso went straight to the interstate. Tears in his eyes
he screamed "I GOT DEM NIGGAS BRO !!!! All of em" he began to

sob uncontrollably and lost control of the car swerving into oncoming traffic nearly missing a unmarked police car . The police car spun around and proceeded to pursue Nutso. When he noticed the lights of the police car behind him Nutso mash down on the accelerator in the attempt to outmaneuver the police. He turned left, then right, doing upwards to 70 mph. He wasn't going back to jail. He loaded his gun with the 100-round drum." Niggas gon have to kill me b" he said through tears.

At that moment a police unit crashed into his side. sending the car into a spiral. Nutso was disorientated from the blow. He managed to get out the car and lifted his gun. Before he could squeeze the trigger, multiple gunshots tore through his body. He was dead before he hit the ground.

Beep Beep Beep... the sound of the heart monitor was the only sound in the hospital beside the shallow breathing of Kills. Connie, Cazz ,Asia and Sasha along with Juice and Na-Na,Kills daughter were all present. He was in a coma for 3 weeks. Butter was nowhere to be found and the shooter was still at large. It was dubbed gang related. The agents that were killed were said to be off duty and just in the wrong place at the wrong time.

Balloons and flowers were in abundance in Kills room.

Kills could hear his family and friends but couldn't find the strength to open his eyes. He kept seeing the gun fire and hearing the bullets fly by. With a deep breath as if it was his first after being submerged underwater Kills open his eyes. Sasha called for a nurse as everyone cheered and tears of joy streamed down their cheeks." Kills welcome back lil bro, thought we lost you" Juice said.

Kills couldn't speak because of the tubes in his mouth and nose. He motioned for Na-na to come to him. As she reached him he squeezed her hand. At that moment the nurse and a Dr. came in and began to remove the tubes. After some tests and questions they left them alone."Sasha take Na-Na home and get some rest" he said to his baby mother. They kissed his cheek and left the room.

"Close the door". He said to Cazz.

"AYO y'all hear anything "? He asked in a frail dry voice.

"Man, the west side papis talkin bout niggas robbed em earlier that night. And it was you". Connie said.

"What"? He asked confused.

"Why they say me if all people"? He asked confused.

"El collar papa" Cazz said.

"Nutso" he said slowly.

"He - he -... gone Pa" Cazz said not wanting to tell him.

His face went blank.

"How "? Was all he said.

"He went to The Capital and shot up Maple and Pond. Then had a shootout with the jakes" Connie explained.

"Y'all seen Butter"? He asked flatly.

"Nobody has... Nubbs locked up Hi got knocked and Lex" Connie said.

"Damn ...." Kills said. He didn't want to tell them anything in the hospital in fear of it being bugged.

"Man, y'all go head imma be good " he instructed.

They all left with instructions to bring the money he owed Nutso to his baby mother 75k wit another 75 as a token of love.

"And no call to or from Butter till I'm home" he said with a deadly stare.

When they left he began plotting his revenge.

"Butter you been on a run for a while now. Setting niggas up. Getting niggas pinched. But now ... it's over,all good things must come to a stop"...

C.A.K.E.
COMING
SOON !!!!

C.A.K.E. II

MORE

CAKE

CAN'T

ALWAYS

KEEP

EVERYTHING

I AM

SALADEEN

Made in the USA
Columbia, SC
16 June 2020